# Just a Passing Phrase I

## Mary Easty

Collated by Richard Easty

First Printing: December 2011

1.0

ISBN 978-1-105-34608-8

# Contents

## Annie Says

*Annie's nephew is getting a bit cheeky — she hopes it's just a passing phrase.*

# Pass the Parcel

I was away for Christmas. I'd had a nice time, but it's always good to get back amongst my friends for New Year. As I got out of the taxi, old Edith Walsh paused in her polishing to wave a welcome from her little house across the road. I was still struggling to get out my keys when I noticed a bottle propped up by my steps, decorated in holly-patterned tissue.

There was a card on a ribbon round its neck but it was quite unreadable. Almost before I had got into the house, my new neighbour from next door came round with some late mail, and we both puzzled over the words, but I gave up and tore off the paper. "Oh dear," I said in disappointment, "I don't recognise this." Diane took the bottle and read the label. "Abendsstein" she said in an annoyingly knowing voice. "This is really good stuff. German, I understand. Very popular this year in Town."

"I wouldn't drink it," I said, "do you want it?" "Oh, yes" she said, "Abendsstein is my thing! It's at all the parties this Christmas."

As she left a little later, bottle in hand, she reminded me about the New Year's party at Kitty's. There was not the slightest reason to think that I might not know about it! Kitty and I had been friends for years, long before Diane had come to live in the Grove. I told her that Kitty relied on me to help every year, specially with my famous cheese patties. Abendsstein wine might not be my thing, I said, but making cheese patties certainly was! I could see that I had scored a point or two there.

On New Year's Eve I went round early to Kitty's. All the Grove would be there, and I helped to set out the chairs and put plates and glasses in their usual party places. Neighbours

1

started to arrive, and as I was popping my cheese patties into Kitty's oven ("Oh, what a lovely welcoming smell!" I heard them saying), I noticed Diane making her entrance. What bright colours some of these young women wear! Then I saw, in her hand, a bottle of wine, in a gold bag with scarlet ribbons! She passed it to Kitty, smiling modestly as she accepted the gushing thanks. As our eyes met, she blushed a little.

I was helping to greet and seat the guests. Grace, from across the Grove, standing near me, was watching Kitty's husband filling the glasses. "That looks an interesting white," she remarked. "It could be an Abendsstein. I hope he doesn't open it for me, but I know who'll soon be after it!" "Really?" I said in surprise. "Oh yes," she said. "Iris. She loves Abendsstein. In fact, I've started to give her a bottle every Christmas." "Where did you discover it?" I asked. "At my own house, actually", Grace told me. "I bought a bottle to give some guests one evening and thought I'd better try it before they arrived, and I asked her to sample it with me. I didn't fancy it myself, but she said it was lovely. So I told her to take it home and that solved my Christmas present for ever! Incidentally," she went on, "could I have another of your wonderful cheese patties? Better than ever this year!"

I walked across to the group Iris was in, and joined in the conversation. When the others moved around, I asked her if she was enjoying the wine she was sipping. "Grace tells me you like Abendsstein," I said. She glanced round to see where Grace was. "It's very awkward," she said. "Actually, this is fizzy lemonade I'm drinking. Abendsstein is dreadful stuff." "But she told me she gives you some every year for Christmas!" "I know! It's so embarrassing!" I passed her another cheese patty and she smiled and made congratulatory noises as she chewed.

2

"What do you do with it?" I was dying to know.

"Well," she confided, "I pass it on to Sylvia down the road. She does love it. She tried some of the first bottle that Grace gave me, we had her and her husband round when they moved in, and they said they liked it. So when I get my Christmas bottle from Grace I wrap it in new paper and give it to Sylvia. She serves it on Christmas day when the family comes!"

"What a very good idea!" I said. "A useful present."

Picking up the last tray of cheese patties, I approached Sylvia. Taking two, "these are delicious!" she enthused, scattering crumbs as she spoke. I smiled and offered "Can I get you a glass of Abendsstein to wash it down?" She almost choked and more crumbs flew over my black frock. "Golly! No thanks! Have you ever touched it? It's vile!" "But Iris was just telling me..." I persevered determined to get to the end of the story. "Oh yes, Iris thinks..." Sylvia was speaking very quietly now and I had to lean towards her to hear. As I leaned, the last few patties began to slide and several people lunged forward to grab them. "I had to try it once, the first time I went to her house. Of course, I had to say it was nice, just to be polite, but I spilt a lot of it on her kitchen floor, and that's when I realised..." "What?" I couldn't wait. "So when she gives you this annual Christmas present, what do you do with it?" Sylvia looked quite guilty, but I could see she was quite pleased with herself. "When it fell on Iris's kitchen floor, all the dirty marks disappeared!" Sylvia was watching my face to see what I thought. "It's most amazing for cleaning tiles and plastic! So I take the bottle round to Edith Walsh, across the road from you, and I put it in her porch, and she cleans the kitchen and mops her floors with it! They all wonder how such an old lady keeps her house so spotless! I hadn't time to take it myself this year, so my nephew dropped it off instead, I hope she found it!" Sylvia and I were both laughing. Iris, Grace, Kitty and Diane were all staring across to see what was amusing us but we just nodded and smiled.

The party broke up soon afterwards. "Don't forget your baking trays," everyone reminded me. "You'll be needing them for next year." As I gathered them up I noticed the Abendsstein, still unopened, on the table. It seemed a pity to leave it there. In a flash I pushed it down amongst my trays, and on my way home I hid the Abendsstein in Edith Walsh's porch.

## Annie Says

*Annie loves to hear Rolf Harris sing "My billabong won't come back."*

# Sheepdrove

In the 1930s, summer was hot sunshine, blue skies, shimmering water...and Sheepdrove, the ramshackle old farm-house where Grandpa and Gran Howarth lived.

Grandpa told us there had been Howarths at Sheepdrove when Adam was a lad, and we could believe him. There were Howarths everywhere around, aunts, uncles and cousins living nearby, and as soon as school broke up, we were all put on the train by our mother and met by Grandpa and for the whole summer we were out on the Downs with the cousins, climbing up Star Hill, ploughing across to Distant Point, all names we made up as we explored. We each carried the picnics Gran gave us, bread, cheese, apples, homemade lemonade in pop bottles, and when we little ones got tired the bigger ones carried us on their shoulders till our strength came back.

In the evenings the families would come to Sheepdrove, the uncles and aunts from the villages, and bring news and gossip, and we would all stay in the garden till we fell asleep. It was great when the young Uncles drove down from town in what we thought were sports cars, trendy in their flannels and open-neck shirts and caps, specially when they brought what Gran and Grandpa called their "beautiful girls" with them, floaty dresses and scarves, silk stockings and high-heeled shoes. Grandpa would bring his gramophone out and wind it up, and the uncles would put on their jazzy music and the "beautiful girls" would kick off their high heels and make us all dance.

Sheepdrove was high up on the Downs, and from the garden sometimes we could see lights across the water. That was France! And we knew the French would be watching us through their telescopes and wishing they could be at Sheepdrove too. Sometimes we were taken across to France and we liked their chips, built English castles on their sand and played football with their children, but we were glad to come home again on the ferry and look up in the hills and think we could see Grandma and Sheepdrove waiting for us.

We thought those summers would last for ever. Some things changed, sometimes a cousin became too grown up to come exploring with us. Sometimes the Aunts handed new babies round for us to cuddle, but the memories blend into each other like a long comfortable roll of film. Except for one year, when I had a strange insight into the grown-up world.

The weather had been very hot for weeks, and as we lounged in the garden, Gran and the Aunts and the Beautiful Girls fanned themselves and the men leaned back in their chairs, Grandpa's beer going down a treat. Somebody glanced across the water and called our attention to the sunset. "Look at the colours!" she said, "so strange, almost green." "Look" we told each other. Clouds were moving slowly across, catching the light, the palest of gleaming pale green. "What colour would you call that?" somebody asked. "Duck-egg?" "Jade?" "and the really dark green?" "Christmas trees!" I said, and everybody laughed, and looked at me, and I felt shy. One of the girls pulled me onto her knee and hugged me and I felt better and snuggled up comfortably. "Definitely a storm coming from France" said one of the Uncles, and as he spoke we heard the first rumbles. The spell was broken. "Thunder!" shouted one of the cousins. "Into the house! Every man for himself!" and they tumbled in, all wanting to crowd under the tin roof to enjoy the noise of the rain. But no rain fell yet, and they soon began a noisy game, and the aunts went in to sort them out, and everyone forgot me, sitting happily and nearly asleep on the girl's knee.

"Certainly coming from France," the uncles spoke more softly amongst themselves, and we watched the flashes far off. Grandpa rescued his treasured gramophone and came back to his chair. The uncles sat quietly, arms round the shoulders of their beautiful girls. "Not thunder, then?" they asked each other. "Afraid not," said Grandpa, "unless you'd call it the thunder of the guns." There was a silence. I, too, kept very still, somehow waiting. "Thunder of the guns from France."

I stirred and sat up, and in surprise they realised I was still there, and looked to see if I had been listening, not knowing that I had heard but not understood. It was long afterwards that I read that phrase again, in a speech made by George Orwell, in the words "The thunder of guns, the jingle of spurs, the catch in the throat when the old flag goes by..." And by then, the world had changed.

# Annie Says

*My friend Annie has been to Ireland, her first time on an aeroplane. She flew Aer Linctus, she told me, and as the plane came in she watched through the window for familiar landmines.*

# All in a Day's Work

I pulled up at the gate and checked my notes. *4pm Mrs White and Raymond (aged four-and-a-half, no speech yet)* it said. The house was the last on the estate, on the edge of the Moor. The winter evening was drawing in and the light was going quickly. As I walked up the path I noticed a primitive tree-house, just a few untidy branches, in one of the many heavy sycamores.

The front door opened before I reached it and a pleasant woman beckoned me in. "How are you with birds?" she asked. Thinking of a budgie I had once had, and the blackbirds I encouraged into my garden, I said "Fine, I think." "Great!" she smiled enthusiastically, and opened an inner door.

The room was quite gloomy and it took me a few seconds to adjust to the scene. Around me I could hear muttering, which at first I thought was the TV, but slowly I began to make out rows of cages, doors wide open, each containing a large bird. Their eyes scanned me from every angle. Mynahs, crows, black and sharp, a magpie, colourful parrots, some I couldn't name, all quite still as they inspected me. Then the rustling and fluttering began again, one or two came out of their cages: I seemed to have been accepted.

Mrs White told me about each bird in turn - its age, name, species - and the birds flew about the room and landed on the various pieces of furniture set around the walls.

After a decent interval, I was able to introduce the reason for my visit. "And Raymond?" I asked. "Where is he?" "Oh, he's always up there," she replied, going to the window. "He takes off whenever I open the door!" I joined her, and we looked out at the tree-house. "What does he do?" I asked.

"He seems to just sit and look out over the Moor," she said. "He gets a very good view, so high up."

"Can you tell me a bit about him before I see him? Has he any brothers or sisters?"

"They're quite a lot older," she said. "They've all left now. When the last one went I got a bit broody!" Empty Nest Syndrome, I thought. She described her seven older children, all good talkers, she said, but Raymond never said a word. "You don't think he's deaf?" I checked. She laughed. "He doesn't miss a thing," she said, and opening the window a tiny slit she suddenly roared "Raymond!"

I jumped. The birds flapped about wildly and as they settled down again a little figure flew into the room. He was small for his age, of slight build, with bright eyes and a big grin. I was astonished at his speed and agility. "You certainly can move fast!" I said to him.

Raymond made no attempt to answer, but came across to perch on the arm of my chair. He had an odd way of staring at me, head on one side, as if listening to something I couldn't hear. I decided to do a few checks, and got out my case.

"Would you like a cup of tea?" asked Mrs White. "I've got some of Raymond's favourite cake, if you're feeling peckish." Somehow I knew it would be seedcake, and Raymond swooped on it with delight.

My checks were quite inconclusive. Raymond seemed to reach the norms for everything but speech. "I'll have to discuss this with the doctors," I told her at last. "I'm sorry not to be of more help, but I'll refer you to someone who will be."

As I closed the gate I looked back. At the window stood Mrs White and Raymond, the last light of the fading day reflected in their faces as they silently watched me.

Behind them shone wings and beaks, and wild beady eyes glinted as the birds moved about in the shadowy room.

When I got back to the clinic I remembered I hadn't asked about Mr White. "Probably flown the coop," I recorded.

# Annie Says

*Annie's neighbour has bad legs. Luckily he's got a nobility badge for his car.*

# Aftermath

The Square was beginning to fill with its usual summer Saturday crowd, shoppers out hunting for bargains, football fans in their bright team colours putting in some sightseeing before the big match. The buskers had set up on their pitches, instrument cases before them to prompt generosity, and the cafés were already spilling tables out around the fountain.

Todd had not far to go for his day's work. He slept in the church doorway each night, and from morning till evening he stood at the end of the nearby passage. Tall and very thin, with plaited, matted rainbow hair and rings in eyebrows and nose, he caught the eye of every passer-by. "Big Issue?" he said.

The day was warm and sunny, and the folk good-natured. Todd was doing quite well. Glancing up as the last stroke of eleven echoed from the church tower, he noticed an unusual movement in the crowd. People were running towards him. He heard a man shouting, and whistles blowing. Gathering up his magazines, he took a step towards the Square to see what was going on. Suddenly there was an enormous explosion, a hideous noise. The ground rocked.

The scene seemed to Todd like a photograph, two-dimensional, no movement, colour or sound. Astounded he stood rigid, his arms still outstretched and his mouth open. After a fraction of a second a terrifying wind rose, whistling round corners, tossing dust and papers, shopping bags and pieces of clothing, and he heard the terrible crash of shattering glass falling in shards like swords, windows sucked out by the vacuum.

As Todd turned, he was struck by a small, compact object blown down the passageway, and was astonished to find a frightened little boy clinging to him, obviously picked up by the wind and flung towards him. Clutching the child in his arms and holding him carefully, Todd ran into the church porch for shelter. Around him there was chaos, people staggering to their feet and racing for cover. Buildings were collapsing, huge chunks of masonry smashing into the pavement. Police were pointing out the escape routes.

As Todd watched, a woman ran out of the passageway, screaming. When she saw the boy tears poured down her face, and seizing him she turned and disappeared. An ambulance-man spoke to Todd: "Well done mate!" "What?" Todd could hardly believe what was happening. "The little lad," said the man, and moved on.

The news of the Manchester bomb flashed round the country almost immediately. In London, a phone rang.

"Mum," an excited voice asked, "have you got the telly on? Well quick – "

Joan switched on and looked at the scenes. She knew why Kate had phoned. "I thought I saw Trevor - talking to an ambulanceman!"

Joan remembered the long months of fruitless searching, the family, their friends, the police, the Salvation Army - the raised hopes, the inevitable despair. All the *sightings*, posters, newspapers. His father had died without ever seeing him again.

Two years had passed - would they even recognise Trevor now? Joan, defending herself against another crushing blow, dared not let herself hope any more. Later Kate rang again, "It was just the way he looked up when the ambulanceman spoke to him," she said. "I thought I might go to Manchester tomorrow and look around a bit." Already Joan could sense the doubts beginning to fill Kate's mind.

When the threat of more bombs could be discounted, teams of hard-hatted workmen cordoned off the most dangerous parts of the Square. Bricks and stones were still dropping, glass covered the whole area. Late that night, the homeless men and women who lived in the passages and doorways crept back. The jagged outlines of the damaged Victorian buildings stood unrecognisable in the moonlight. As Todd pulled his blankets round him, his thoughts returned to the child who had literally fallen into his arms. The mother's face kept appearing before him as he drifted in and out of sleep.

Towards morning, he packed his belongings together and counted his money. Taking a last long look around, as if to imprint this picture in his memory for ever, he turned and left the Square.

# Annie Says

*Annie would love to be young again, footsore and fancy free.*

# The Fortune Teller

The fortune teller gazed into the crystal ball, then looked long and hard at me. It was obvious she had much to reveal, and I was determined to learn everything from her. How did she create this feeling of mystery, this excitement, this trust? The room was dark, lit only by one or two subtly-placed lamps which emphasised the glowing, hypnotic crystal on the table between us. Incense burners scented the shadows, and their smoke trailed a curling haze reflected in the many mirrors.

The fortune teller took my hands but held herself away from me, her body clothed in flowing silky garments, black and silver chiffon covering her hair and much of her face. Quiet music enhanced the stillness.

As I drank in the heady atmosphere, she began to speak. Her voice was low and melodious and her words came slowly, sometimes with great emphasis – *luck – money – a stranger – long life* – and sometimes dipping so that the meaning eluded me and faded away with the mist. As she stroked my fingers she talked about my marriage, and she seemed to study my face keenly when she touched on age and past experiences. The burning crystal mesmerised me, and when I tore my eyes away from it her intense stare drew me back to her face: I seemed to be drifting between the two, her urgent voice entrancing me.

Suddenly she jumped to her feet. The spell shattered, I leapt up too. "God, Doris!" she cried. "Look at the time!" She tore off her black nylon dressing-gown and threw it towards me. My shaking fingers tied the belt round my waist and fastened the shawl round my head. Checking the incense (another tablet, a hasty match) and winding the cassette tape back, she said, "Just remember, speak slowly, romance, money, health, you know! I'll be as quick as I can! Oh, I hope I'm not too late! I never know whether he'll be there!"

She shot off through a curtain and, trembling, I took her place in the shadows as the door opened and a nervous middle-aged woman came in, clutching a large handbag.

"Thank goodness!" I thought, "it's that widow from the cake shop who has just started going bowling with Bert from the garage."

As she sank into the chair opposite mine, I took a deep breath. I gazed into the crystal ball, then looked long and hard at her.

# Annie Says

*Annie's friends have asked her to go to the opera with them. She thinks it's called "The Magic Fruit."*

# Hello, Dolly! Incident In Bridge Street

Dolly checked her watch as she turned into Bridge Street — fifty minutes before the car would be at the door to pick her up! She stumbled into the hall, dropped her bag onto the table and started up the stairs, but almost immediately the kitchen door opened, Len silhouetted in the doorway. She scowled, and as he said the inevitable "Hello, Dolly!" she mouthed it with him, sour-faced.

"I've no time to waste," she warned him. "I'm in a rush!"

"What's new?" he replied easily. "I'll be out soon myself. I'll get something to eat later."

Without showing any further interest he returned to his newspaper. Dolly raced up the stairs, peeling off layers as she ran, throwing her clothes into the linen basket, turning on the bathroom taps. She had just settled amongst the scented bubbles when Len called, "Don't do anything I wouldn't do!" and the front door slammed behind him.

"Anything you wouldn't do!" she thought. What had Len ever done? All the doing in their marriage had been hers. They had both started at Nixon's Mill straight from school, him in the machine shop and herself in the cutting-room. Dead-end jobs, everyone worked there, but she had seen her chance when "young" Mr Nixon joined the family firm. Dolly had watched him walking round amongst the girls, an arm round this one, a sly pinch for that, and planned her moves. Nixon's Mill meant clothes, didn't it? She had always made her own things, so she took care now to choose the brightest colours, the tightest-fitting and most daring styles, and it worked!

Promotion followed rapidly, and Dolly could ignore the giggles and gossip. Over the years, Young Mr Nixon became

"Niko". Dolly, renamed Dolores, was his Personal Assistant, and with Niko's money and Dolores' ambition, they brought in famous designers, the most well-known models, and Nixon's Mill became Niko's Fashion House, one of the Top Three, making a fortune throughout the world of Haute Couture. As Dolores, her clothes were hand made by the best seam-stresses in the House, she had front-row seats at all the parades, she led the applause when Niko's models minced down the cat- walk. On Niko's arm she attended the pre-show cocktail parties and the post-show dinners, stayed in the world's best hotels with him and made many of the manage-ment decisions that he announced. Len refrained from com-ment, as well he might, she thought - he enjoyed the extra money, though he would never agree to move from Bridge Street to a grander address.

Time was passing as she soaked and reminisced, she must prepare for the evening. Exquisite silk underwear was waiting on the bed, the new scarlet dress hanging on the wardrobe door. A quick flick of her hairbrush - the firm's own stylist would be waiting for her at the hotel - and she applied her make-up lightly and fastened the firm's diamonds round her neck. She eased on her high-heeled shoes and walked carefully downstairs. The fifty minutes were almost up. She buttoned up her black velvet jacket and checked her reflection in the long glass.

As she opened the front door, she noticed an envelope, propped up on the table. "Now what can Len want?" she grumbled, slipping it into her bag.

The uniformed chauffeur picked up her overnight case, monogrammed with the firm's logo. As he opened the door of the long grey limousine and handed her in, they were both well aware that in the shadows behind the dark windows of Bridge Street the neighbours would be watching the scene. In the bright street lights illuminating the car like a stage set, the chauffeur presented Dolores with a large bouquet. "From Mr Niko, Madame," he said. Dolores smiled gracefully and bent to breathe in the scent of the flowers, as she always did at this point, and the audience sighed at such luxury.

But he had something else to say: "Mr Niko sends his regrets, Madame - he will not be staying at the Regis tonight".

"Not -" Dolores began, her heart suddenly thumping - and the smooth voice continued. "The parade tomorrow will be at the Lyonesse, and I am to take you there in the morning to meet him."

He touched his cap and slid into his seat. As the engine responded to his touch he glanced through his mirror.

Dolores' mouth had settled into a hard line. So this had been a surprise? he thought. She hadn't noticed the clues? He smiled inwardly and gave her an appraising look. She was still a beautiful woman. . .

Dolores took a deep breath and stared ahead as the car picked up speed and swung out of Bridge Street, so she didn't notice the couple watching from the unlit house opposite.

"She's gone!" said the woman. "She can't have read your letter!" "What's new?" said Len, picking up their cases and making for the door.

"We've done our best - now let's get on with the rest of our lives."

# A Country Life: Sylvia

Sylvia grew up in the city with her brothers and sisters. Above the busy streets and concrete buildings, the sodium lights on top of the Mission drew the people like moths to a candle. Sylvia first met Matt there, and was enchanted to find that he was a farmer. She had learnt about farms at the Mission, and knew about seed-time and harvest, and the fruits of the earth. She had heard about ploughing and scattering, and could imagine the beauty of the fields of golden corn. She knew that farmers' wives and their chubby, healthy children handed out home-made pies and plum cake to the suntanned farm-hands at the Harvest Home.

The Mission held a Harvest Festival every autumn, when everyone bought extra bread and fruit from the corner shop and arranged it on the platform. One year Sylvia's sister took a tin of beans for the vegetable shelf. Some people laughed, but the lady from "Help the Aged" said the pensioners would be glad.

For the last 20 years, Sylvia and Matt have lived on a farm at Piebold Fen. Fens are reclaimed land, drained and channelled to sustain agriculture. Sylvia too is drained and channelled and sustains agriculture. She works alongside her husband, driving his machinery, digging, lifting, loading. She lives amongst vegetables. The only animals are the thin, malevolent cats.

Piebold Fen really is in the middle of nowhere. The flat-earthers would be comfortable there. From the farmhouse the grey sullen fields stretch away west towards the sea, east towards the city, south towards the railway lines and north towards the canal. None of these can be seen from the farm, even with binoculars from the attic windows. Herons hunt along the drains, the farm cats stalk among the reeds, the ever-present mist encircles the cringing cabbages.

Sylvia's two sons are grown-up now. The older one works in a transport office in the city, cherishes his motor-bike and follows United. The younger son has all but disappeared: left home as soon as he finished at the local school, took nothing with him and has not been seen since. Sylvia knows he is alive, because the money she puts into his account is taken out regularly. The Bank is Not Allowed to Disclose Any Information about its Customers.

Sylvia used to love the Mission, specially the hymns. Verses that rhymed, went with a good rhythm, preferably with a thumping chorus. She can still remember lots of them and chants them to herself as she pedals back off the road and along the interminable pebbled path with her shopping bags. Sometimes the cats slink through the rows of cabbages and follow her.

Matt goes to bed earlier and earlier these days. When he has gone, Sylvia reaches for her exercise book and writes down her own hymns. In the silence, the words pour out and shout to her from the page. Sometimes it is almost dawn before she stops and draws a careful line, with the knowledge that she has gathered in enough to face the new day.

# The Boy Who Lived in the Sky

On the first day that Danny went to school, Miss Roberts asked him where he lived. It was Miss Roberts' first day, too, and seemed a good question to ask. "Up in the sky," he said, smiling at her. "Right," said Miss Roberts. "So, Danny how do you get to school?" And he said "First we fly down to the ground, and then we walk round the corner." "Right,"said Miss Roberts, and when his Mum came to meet him, Miss Roberts went out into the playground and told her what he had said.

"Well, yes!" said Danny's Mum. "He's quite right, really. You see that tall tower block behind the market? The only one left now? Danny and the baby and I live on the top floor, we've not been rehoused yet, and it is up in the sky! Through the front window we can see the hills, but from the bedroom window at the back we can only see grey concrete, ledges and drain pipes, so we keep the curtains closed. It's very cramped, two rooms, but that's where we live."

"Danny says you fly down," said Miss Roberts.

"We all get in the lift, with our bags and the baby's trolley, and Danny pushes the button which says 'ground' and the lift bumps and falls and jolts just as if we are flying," said Danny's Mum.

Miss Roberts laughed and gave Danny a hug. "See you tomorrow," they all said.

Every day Danny met his Mum and the baby at the school gate. One day he was very excited. "One of the boys has got a dog!" he announced. "His Mum brought it to show us. Miss Roberts said it's very good to have a dog for a friend." "Oh, yes," said his Mum. "So can I have one?" asked Danny. "I'd like a dog to be my friend."

His Mum felt sad. She knew it was lonely for Danny, living so high up. There were no other children left in the tower, and he couldn't go out to play, like other children, he couldn't go up and down on his own yet, and make friends. Some times she saw him watching through the window seeing other children playing together in the streets and gardens far away. "We couldn't have a dog up here," she said. "There isn't room in the flat, there's not really enough room for the pram, we couldn't let him out. I'm sorry, Dan, there's no chance we could have a dog."

The next day Dan came back with another idea.

"Mum!" he said. "One of the boys has a kitten. It's so small it fits into his hand!" He held out his own little fat hand to show her. "It was lovely. Miss Roberts likes people to have cats too. She says everyone should have a pet."

"Poor Dan," thought his Mum, and for a moment almost gave in. Then common sense prevailed. "Look, Dan cats have to be outside a lot of the time, they don't like to stay in a little room." Dan was beginning to understand that Miss Roberts didn't mean everybody.

Then it was rabbits, but even Danny could see that there was no room for rabbits. His Mum was wondering what else Miss Roberts would suggest. Snakes? Ferrets?

However, when Dan came out of school next day, his Mum was looking very pleased with herself, as though she had a nice secret to surprise him with. "You wait till we get home," she told him. "I've something to show you." For a heady moment dogs, cats, rabbits, mice all passed before his eyes and he skipped along beside the rattling trolley, but when they got in there was nothing to see.

Disappointed, he followed her into the bedroom to change

22

out of his school uniform. The curtain was drawn back, which was unusual. "Look out there, Dan," said his Mum.

Dan looked out at the grey concrete walls, the ledges, the drain pipes, and then he looked again. A big bird, reddish brown with spots and lines on its back and a long tail, was sitting just outside the window, close to a pipe, pieces of straw and grass in its beak. "What is it? What's it doing?" Dan whispered. "I think it's building a nest," said his Mum, and she showed him her book and pointed to a picture, "It's just like this. I think it's called a kestrel." Danny gazed open-mouthed, and even the baby was quiet.

The bird flew away, and Dan almost cried. "It's gone!" he worried. "No," said his mum, "I've been watching it all day. Just look, where it was sitting, it's making a nest. It's fetching more sticks." They held their breath as the kestrel returned, just as she had said. "Will it stay for a bit?" Dan asked hopefully. "When the nest is ready it will lay some eggs, and then there will be some baby birds to watch."

"Oh, Mum! The kestrels can be my pets!" cried Dan joyfully. He drew a picture to take to school, and Miss Roberts showed it to the class. "I've got the best pet of all!" he said. "Yes," said Miss Roberts, "You are a very lucky boy. The boy and his bird who live in the sky."

# Anonymous

Andy Taylor was one of the members of our writing group. He had been a member for four or five years — we hadn't realised it was so long until we got his letter of resignation, a quiet, understated note that exactly reflected its writer. At our meetings he read out his short homeworks so quietly that we had to lean forward and concentrate keenly to follow the drift; diffident classwork that never revealed any emotion, careful comments (when prompted) which never expressed an opinion. In a strange sort of way, I suppose, we sheltered him, anxious not to cause offence to such an inoffensive soul.

He didn't give any reason for leaving, and the letter ended rather clumsily, "perhaps you may see me about" rather than the more usual "hope to see you around," But there again, we wouldn't have said anything about it, would never do anything to hurt his feelings; and, in fact, we wondered (feeling mean) would we be sure to recognise him if we DID see him about? What had he looked like? Average size, average age, colouring, clothes, expression — that was our Andy Taylor! Got on with us all for four years, and nobody could describe him! We settled down again, welcomed a new member to sit in his chair, and the gap filled up like a pond when a frog jumps out.

Then one evening, one of our group phoned me. "Are you watching BBC one? The stars arriving at the film premiere?" I switched over hurriedly from the rugby, ignoring the strangled cries of my men. Women like stick insects in gorgeous frocks were sashaying along the red carpet into the London theatre. My eye fell on a figure by the staircase. He turned with a welcoming kiss for Catherine Zeta, and in a flash I (almost) identified our Andy. The name, Andrew Taylor, director, passed in the confusion, and he was gone.

A week or so later, flicking through the sports channels, I could have sworn I saw him again! Sue Barker was interviewing Willie Carson at Ascot. Willie was wobbling on his box, and as the camera swung towards him (cruelly) to expose his predicament, a winning jockey rode triumphantly into the paddock. Celebrating amongst the owners and hangers-on, wearing the racing man's regulation raincoat and snappy trilby pulled at an angle over his face, was an ecstatic figure . . . The caption read Andrew Tailor, trainer.

By now, many of us were sure we had seen Our Andy on TV. As "Drew Taylor" he shook champagne into a fountain in the back row of the Chelsea team photo on Cup Final day, and as "Taylor Drew" he threw his tennis shoes into the crowd when out-played by Federer at the French Open.

Still abroad, we were not all convinced that he was the rider sporting the yellow jersey coming over the highest mountain pass on the Italian border. The camera was rather jumpy, but it looked very like him, standing up on the pedals, arms in the air, yelling with triumph and then with pain as he collided with over-eager spectators. Andre le Tailleur, the commentator called him through his Gallic crocodile tears.

Several of us watched avidly, but we could not be certain whether he took part in the London marathon. There were so many bearded nuns, but as they flashed by somebody from Blue Peter called "Hi, Andy!" and hauled a breathless sister-of-mercy to one side for an interview, only to be engulfed under the unrelenting wave upon wave of runners.

The appearances built up. A man who looked like a rather flustered version of Andy Taylor was ejected in the first round of "The Apprentice". We were mortified when Sir Alan Sugar roared at him, "You claim to be an under-writer? You couldn't write your own name! You're FIRED!"

And then there was the nasty incident with the sheep in "One Man and His Dog"...

"Spotting Our Andy" became quite a competition for us, and we spent much more time watching TV than we did on our homework. The phones were hot with our calls, and we developed a sophisticated signalling system to save bills, four rings for Channel 4, 3, 2, 1 etc.

The whole thing ended abruptly.

One Friday as we were just starting our meeting, Andy Taylor walked in! We froze - and nobody spoke, then all at once we began our polite greetings, "Hello, Andy!" "How are you?" "So nice to see you," with pauses where we hoped he might "tell all" filled with tactful welcomes "good to have you back!" "Good to be back", he replied quietly, shyly, with a little shrug. Of course, nobody asked him any direct question, we didn't like to, didn't want to pry or make him feel uncomfortable. So he sat down on the nearest vacant chair and read out his homework, in his modest, self-effacing way, never catching anyone's eye. "Anonymous," it was called. We all leaned forward and concentrated politely.


# Annie Says

*Annie's son has a very technical job at a firm in Newcastle, in charge of non-ferocious metals.*

# The Door Was Open

Sweating foot-soldiers strained against the heavy oak, and with a great crash the sleeping countryside burst into chaos. A line of horses charged under the huge stone archway, the outriders low in the saddle, banners held high, brilliant light dazzling on their breastplates. Then came rows of marching men, dust clouds rising as their boots stamped steadily on the thirsty path, keeping time to the beat of a single drum.

Amongst the troops rattled the crested black coach, the driver carefully controlling his ponies. And in the coach was the Lady: elegant, austere, proud and beautiful, head thrown back on her long white neck as she passed under the arch, eyes scanning as if for the last time the inscription carved above, the motto of her ancestors who had lived in the castle for centuries. Slowly her lips formed the inspirational words. Languidly she used her fan against the summer heat, then, resting her arm on the sill, turned to look at the familiar fields, her face sad and drawn.

The coach passed and along came more horsemen. The procession rounded the bend and was gone. Silence returned, the path empty, the sound of boots and hooves dying away.

Then one by one, figures emerged from the hawthorn hedges, climbed out of the deep dry ditches and gathered by the door. One of them was a small man with a sun-browned face, chewing a cigar, headphones pulled down round his neck. He stood staring down the lane. A taller, thinner man, hopping over the brambles, spoke to him. "Whadya think, Reggie?"

Reggie grunted. I shall record Reggie's conversation rather than quote it, to avoid the use of continual dashes which waste

27

so much time and paper. Reggie indicated that he was not happy. Sid bent to pick prickles from his trousers, to conceal his desperate expression. Not again!

Others were approaching now, wiping dirty faces on their sleeves, some carrying heavy equipment, rolling up electric wires. The soldiers were shambling back down the lane, too tired for conversation, the bright uniforms clogged with agricultural powder. They flung themselves down on the grass and covered their red faces with their caps. "Tinnies" appeared from back pockets, gum pushed through parched lips. Teenagers from "wardrobe" frantically gathered up pieces of armour. The horses were led into a field and settled down to nibble and crunch.

Reggie raised himself to his full 5ft6, loud hailer to his lips, and announced that he was not satisfied. He explained how very much he was not satisfied, and why. The men round him flinched. At this point the coach rolled back, pushed by four or five hands, the ponies having been first in the field. The Lady stumbled out, skirts clutched at waist height, thick trainers sticking to the sandy ground. A bottle was retrieved from under her shawl and she drank noisily, her head (as before) tilted back on her swan-like neck. This familiar piece of action set off Reggie again. "As for you —"he screeched. The Lady gave him a withering look — the best acting for days. "Don't forget the family motto!" muttered a weary wag, hoping for a diversion. The Lady rose to the challenge, mouthing the words as though the cameras were still rolling. "Nobbles O'Bligg" the Lady sneered. "Whoever he is." "Latin," said Sid. She lit a cigarette, throwing carton and match into the rambling roses, which being made of plastic smouldered with a chemical smell, and with a well-chosen phrase shuffled off. Reggie too was smouldering.

Then came Reggie's revenge.

Beckoning Sid towards him, he addressed him through his quivering loud-hailer, then turned and strode off through the door.

Sid faced the hostile crowd, and passed on the message. "On yer feet! Action stations! As you were! Start in 20!" inwardly groaning, "God! Not again??"

After a dreadful moment when Sid (and Reggie too, if he were to be truthful) feared a rebellion, the men trudged back through the archway, coach and animals returned to their marks. The sun glared unforgivingly down, lines were formed, the Lady pinned up her hair and leaned back against the cushions. For a blissful moment, the silence held. The door was closed — waiting. . .

# Annie Says

*When Annie was ill, she was glad of her telephone. She said it was her only contact with the other world.*

www.ingramcontent.com/pod-product-compliance
Lightning Source LLC
Chambersburg PA
CBHW071629140626
46555CB00021B/1886